My John 3:16 Book

Lola Mazola's
HAPPYLAND ADVENTURE

written by
Robert J. Morgan

pictures by
Glin Dibley

B&H
PUBLISHING GROUP
Nashville Tennessee

MY JOHN 3:16 BOOK

ISBN: 978-0-8054-4634-0

B&H Publishing Group

Nashville, Tennessee

BHPublishingGroup.com

Dewey Decimal Classification: F

Subject Heading: Salvation-Fiction / Regeneration (Christianity)-Fiction

Printed in Singapore

1 2 3 4 11 10 09 08

To Chloe

A Word To Adults

This is no ordinary book. Think of it as a do-it-yourself handbook for leading your child to Christ through the doorway of John 3:16.

My John 3:16 Book explains this enduring verse phrase-by-phrase in the context of a story that illustrates its truths. And the suggested prayer at the end of the book can guide your child to receive Christ's salvation and everlasting life.

Watch for a teachable moment, pray, and find a time when your children are alert and responsive. Read this book with them, discussing its story.

Many youngsters will then be ready to pray the prayer at the end of this book as their own.

Don't pressure your children to receive Christ, but be ready to encourage them if they seem interested. Afterward, have them sign their names and register the date in the provided space.

The simple act of scribbling name and date in a book is crucial. Many Christians receive Christ in childhood but later can't remember just when and where. Some subsequently question the validity of their decision. Others, not doubting their conversion, regret their vague recollection of it. As long as your children live, they will cherish the dated signature in the book as a priceless keepsake.

May the Lord bless you and your child with a personal knowledge of His one and Only Son, and of the everlasting life He lovingly gives.

Lola's dark eyes examined the travel folder.
Her left cheek felt a trickling tear.

"Please, daddy," she begged. "The Motleys are taking a trip.
They are going to Happyland. And they want me to go with
them! Happyland has
**60 RIDES, 20 SHOWS,
3 HOTELS, 2 LAKES,**
a **WATERPARK,**
and a **ZOO!**

"Please, daddy,
can't I go?
Please?"

She looked from her folder to her father. He seemed sad. "I'm sorry, honey," he said. "You need $95 for the trip. I don't have that much. Do you have any money in your bubble bank?"

Lola ran to her room. She twisted the bottom from her bank. She shook out her coins. She had three dollars and thirty-seven cents. "Humm," said Mr. Mazola, putting his finger to his forehead. "Perhaps I can sell one of my paintings tomorrow."

The next day, he took his paintings to the park. Many people admired them. Several said he was a good painter. Three people said he was a wonderful painter. One said he was the best painter in the world.

But nobody bought a painting.

That night, Lola Mazola cried herself to sleep.

The next day was Sunday. Lola and her father went to Sunday School. Her uncle, Tom Tweed, was the teacher.

"Let's study the most famous verse in the Bible," he said.

"That's John 3:16!" said Lola.

"That's right," said Mr. Tweed.

For God loved the world in this way: He gave His One and Only Son, so that everyone who believes in Him will not perish but have eternal life.

Mr. Tweed explained the verse like this:

For God . . .

Who is God?

God is the one who made the heavens and the earth.
He made light and night, land and sea, sun and moon.
He also made the stars.

He made trees and plants. Bees and ants.
And fleas and seas and knees and peas.
And bumblebees
and chimpanzees.

He made everything.

He even made you and me.

God is invisible. We can't see Him. But He is everywhere.
He knows everything. He can do anything.
He cares for everyone. Every day.
He even loves you and me.

For God loved the world . . .

What is the world?

It is planet earth. A huge round ball, spinning in space.

Planet earth is full of woods and waters.
Fish and otters.
Dogs and cats.
Mice and rats.
Birds and bats.
Flies and gnats.
And people.

Special people like you.

God loves people like you very much.
He loves you so much He has given you a special gift.

For God loved the world in this way: He gave His One and Only Son . . .

Who is God's Son? God's Son is Jesus, born on Christmas Day in a barn in Bethlehem. He was wrapped in rags and laid in a heap of hay.

Jesus grew up in a little town called Nazareth.
He helped His mother Mary clean house.
He helped His father Joseph build furniture.
He studied in the school and splashed in the stream.
He played in the park and prayed in the temple.

He never disobeyed His parents.
Or lost His temper.
Or hurt a friend.
He never cheated.
He never lied.

He was perfect.
Perfectly perfect.

When Jesus was thirty years old, He left Nazareth.
He traveled from town to town, walking and talking,
teaching and preaching.

He stilled the storms
and healed the sick.
He amazed the crowds
and raised the dead.

**He was perfect.
Perfectly perfect.**

One day some evil people captured Jesus. They made fun of Him. They tied Him up and beat Him up.

They nailed His hands and feet to a cross-shaped post. They wanted to kill Him. They did kill Him.

They laughed as He died.

His friends took Him down from the cross.

They buried Him in a cave.
He wasn't breathing.
He wasn't moving.
His heart was stopped.
His eyes were closed.

He was dead. Perfectly dead.

But He didn't stay that way!
Three days later, the cave was empty.
Jesus was alive again!
His eyes were open.
His heart was beating.
His lungs were breathing.

He returned to life!

Why did Jesus die and return to life?

For God loved the world in this way: He gave His One and Only Son, so that everyone who believes in Him will not perish . . .

What does it mean to perish? God doesn't want us to stay on planet earth forever. He has a happier world than this one. He wants us to be together forever with Him and with our family and friends in His happy land. God's happy land is called Heaven. The light is brighter there. The sky is bluer. The air is sweeter. The land is neater. The people nicer.

No one ever sighs there. No one ever lies there.
No one cries there. Nor dies there.

**It's perfect.
Perfectly perfect.**

To perish means never
getting to go to God's
happy land.

Why would we not be able to go to God's happy land? Because we have all broken God's rules in the Bible. We disobey our parents. We lose our temper. We hurt our friends. We cheat. We lie. We are not perfectly perfect.

But since Jesus died on the cross, God can forgive us for breaking His rules in the Bible. Then we can go to His perfect place.

How do we receive this gift?

For God loved the world in this way: He gave His One and Only Son, so that everyone who believes in Him will not perish but have eternal life.

What does it mean to believe in Him?

it means . . .

To believe that Jesus is God's One and Only son.
To believe that He was born in Bethlehem.
To believe that He died and returned to life.
To believe that He can forgive us for disobeying God.

it means . . .

To believe it enough to obey Him.
To believe it enough to talk to Him in prayer.

it means . . .

To pray something like this:

Dear God, I believe that Jesus died and rose again.
Please forgive me for breaking your rules in the Bible.
Help me obey you. I want Jesus to be my Best Friend.
I want to live some day in Your happy land of Heaven.

Mr. Tweed then gave each child a little sign with the words of John 3:16 printed in happy colors. Lola showed it to her dad as they left Sunday School. "I'm going to hang it on my mirror," she said, "as soon as I get home."

But she forgot. She saw her travel folder of Happyland, and she started looking at it. She studied it all afternoon. She thought of the . . .

60 RIDES, 20 SHOWS,
3 HOTELS, 2 LAKES,
a **WATERPARK,**
and a **ZOO**!

Oh, how she wanted to go to Happyland! Her left cheek felt a trickling tear. And she forgot all about John 3:16.

Then the doorbell rang.

Uncle Tom Tweed had come to visit.

"Hi, Lola," he said. "I can't stay. I'm in a hurry.
But I have a gift for you. It's a super-duper surprise!"

His eyes twinkled as he handed Lola a card.

"Don't open it till I'm gone," he said.
He turned to leave.

"Thank you," Lola called after him.

Then she shut the door
and opened the card.

Dear Lola,

I love you very much. So much that I'm giving you a gift of $100. Now you won't have to miss your trip. You can go to Happyland after all! Have a wonderful time.

Love, Uncle Tom.

A $100 bill was taped to the card.

"Daddy!" Lola shouted. "Uncle Tom gave me $100! Now I can go to Happyland! I can go! I can really go!"

Lola ran around the room.
She jumped in the air
and hugged her father till his neck hurt.

That evening, Lola's dad helped her pack.

"Lola," he said, sitting on her bed, "your Uncle Tom loved you enough to give his own money so that you would not miss your trip, but could go to Happyland."

"Yes," said Lola. "It's the nicest thing anyone has ever done for me."

"Not quite," said her dad. "I know someone who has done something even better."

"Who?" Lola asked.

"God," said Mr. Mazola, opening his Bible.

"John 3:16 says that God loved Lola Mazola in this way: He gave His One and Only Son, so that if Lola will believe in Him, she will not perish but will have eternal life."

Lola snuggled closer to her dad.

"Uncle Tom gave his money so that you could go to Happyland for a week. But God gave His One and Only Son so that you could go to His happy land of Heaven forever. You were glad to accept Uncle Tom's gift. Would you like to accept God's special gift, too?"

They talked a while longer. Then Lola knelt by her bed and prayed:

Dear God, I believe that Jesus died and rose again.
Please forgive me for breaking your rules in the Bible.
Help me obey you. I want Jesus to be my Best Friend.
I want to live some day in Your happy land of Heaven.
In Jesus' Name, Amen.

Lola felt happy.
Her dad felt very happy.
His left cheek felt a
trickling tear.
They hugged each
other till their
necks hurt.

They finished packing.
Lola snuggled into bed.
Her dad said good night
and turned off the light.
The glow from the moon
filled the room.

Lola was too happy to sleep.
She looked at the ceiling.
She looked at the floor.
She looked at the wall.
The she remembered!

**What did Lola
remember?**

She . . .

She remembered . . .

She remembered her sign.

She slid from her bed and found it.

She taped it to her mirror, then crawled back into bed.

Her dark eyes examined it a long, long time.

Its bright words seemed just for her.

They were just for her.

And they are

for you,

too.

For God loved the world in this way: He gave His One and Only Son, so that everyone who believes in Him will not perish but have eternal life.

Would you like to believe in Jesus?

Would you like to receive God's wonderful gift?
If so, take a moment now, bow your head, and pray
this prayer out loud as your own.

Lola did.

Dear God, I believe that Jesus died and rose again. Please forgive me for breaking your rules in the Bible. Help me obey you. I want Jesus to be my Best Friend. I want to live some day in your happy land of Heaven. In Jesus' Name, Amen.

Signed_____

Date_____

Now What?

Asking Jesus to be your best friend is the most important thing you will ever do. But now you need to grow stronger as His friend and follower. How can you do that?
Here are four big ways:

1. Read your Bible every day and memorize some of its verses. You might start by learning John 3:16!

2. Pray every day.

3. Tell others about Jesus.

4. Go to Sunday School and church each week.

Being a Christian is exciting, but sometimes hard.
Make up your mind to love and obey Jesus all the time,
no matter what.

And may God bless you every day.

Robert J. Morgan is a best-selling Gold Medallion Award-winning author, a staff writer for Dr. David Jeremiah's Turning Points Magazine, and has also served as pastor of The Donelson Fellowship in Nashville, Tennessee, for the past twenty-seven years. He holds degrees from Columbia International University (B.S.), Wheaton Graduate School (M.A.), and Luther Rice Seminary (M.Div.).

Glin

When **Glin Dibley** is not drawing or painting wacky children's books, he's out coaching and playing soccer with his two girls. He has illustrated more than twenty covers for publishers such as Knopf, Harper Collins, and Scholastic and has finished a few books including: It's a Bad Day, Don't Laugh at Me, and Kid Tea. His studio is right by the beach in Huntington Beach where you can find him surfing with his buddies. Glin is the only boy in a house full of girls; his wife and two girls, a girl dog and a girl hamster.

Make sure to visit **LolaMazola.com** for fun Lola Mazola projects you can download.